# Juana & Lucas
# BIG PROBLEMAS

# Juana & Lucas

## BIG PROBLEMAS

JUANA MEDINA

CANDLEWICK PRESS

Much gratitude to Christopher Kardambikis, Gillian MacKenzie,
my dear family, and my team *maravilla* at Candlewick.

• • •



First edition 2019

Library of Congress Catalog Card Number 2018961934
ISBN 978-1-5362-0131-4

19 20 21 22 23 24 CCP 10 9 8 7 6 5 4 3 2 1

Printed in Shenzhen, Guangdong, China

This book was typeset in Nimrod and Avenir.
The illustrations were done in ink and watercolor.

Candlewick Press
99 Dover Street
Somerville, Massachusetts 02144

visit us at www.candlewick.com

To my cousins, new and old.

To Piti.

To the thoughtful boy in Central Falls, RI,
who inspired this book.

# CHAPTER 1

My name is Juana. I live in Bogotá, Colombia, with my two most favorite people in the world: Mami and my dog, Lucas.

# *My life is just about perfect.*
# PERFECT.
## And here's why:

I live in a city that smells of eucalyptus and fresh fruit and has beautiful mountains. My home overlooks the city, so I can see when the city is awake and—if I'm awake past bedtime—when it goes to sleep.

We have the nicest neighbors, Mr. and Mrs. Sheldon. I am always welcome in their home, as long as I take off my muddy sneakers before I step on their carpet.

Mami is also perfect. Except when I do something that gets me into trouble. Then her eyes turn the greenest green and she says my full name, *Juana Medina Rosas,* and to go to her *inmediatamente.* That's not perfect. But overall, Mami is pretty fantastic.

My *abuelos* are about the most wonderful people that have ever existed, and they have existed for a very long time!

My school is quite good, too, even though math and English are hard for me to learn. Mr. Tompkins might call me out every now and then for getting in trouble, but that's okay, too. (Staying quiet AND still are not my specialties.)

The number one most perfect thing of all things in my life is **LUCAS.**

He is the most perfect *perro* in the whole entire world. Despite being neurotic, eating my homework, and snoring, he is **the best of *amigos.***

Lately, *mi vida* has become a little less perfect.

Some days ago, Mami came to pick me up from school and I got into the car. But when I looked up, I thought I was in the wrong car with the wrong Mami. Her hair looked completely different.

Mami's old hair was excellent. That's the truth. So I told her I liked her old hair way better. She wasn't too happy about my comment. That's when I knew I was in the right car with the right Mami, just not with the right hairdo. I don't know why she had to fluff it and fancy it up.

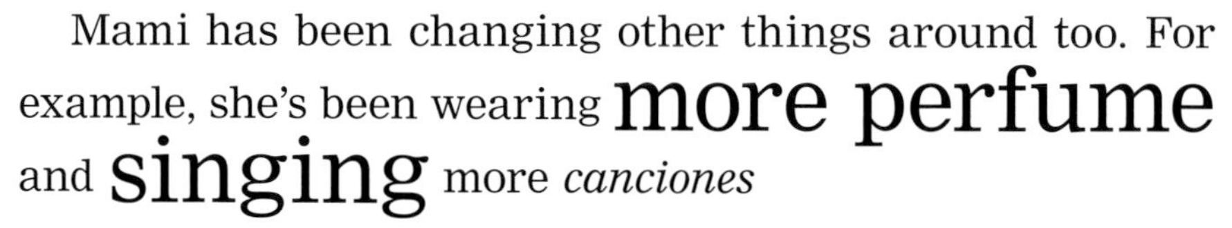

Mami has been changing other things around too. For example, she's been wearing **more perfume** and **singing** more *canciones*

and wearing more

**lipstick.**

I think her perfume is nice, but not so nice that she should wear a lot of it. Also, it makes Lucas sneeze! Lipstick might be fun, but it also means that getting ready to go anywhere takes longer. I think it's best when it doesn't take so long, especially when Mami is supposed to be bringing me to my *abuelos'* or to Piti's.

# CHAPTER 2

## I love spending time with Piti!

Lately, I've been visiting her a lot. Piti is my *abuelo*'s sister. Her real name is Cecilia, but we all call her Piti because it's shorter.

# *There are many things I like about spending time with Piti.*

MANY. THINGS.

And here are a few:

# Ajiaco *is my favorite soup.* FAVORITE.
And here's why:

*Ajiaco* is a creamy soup made with many types of potatoes. Some are soft and become liquid. Some are hard and stay in chopped pieces, even after hours of boiling on the stove top.

*Ajiaco* also has *maíz.* The cob can be hard to fish out of the soup, and the big, salty kernels can make a splashy mess.

It has capers, which are like green polka dots in a sea of creamy potatoes.

There's always a sweet slice of fresh avocado sitting like a canoe on top of the soup.

Chicken and sour cream and green herbs make the soup not only taste delicious but smell fantastic.

Eating *ajiaco* is like giving my tummy a warm hug.

# CHAPTER 3

If I don't stay with my *abuelos* or with Piti, I'll stay with my two cousins, who are the best. Their names are Cami and Pipe. Their dad is my favorite uncle. His name is Guillermo, but we call him Memo.

Sometimes my cousins live with Memo, and sometimes they live with their mom. Cami and Pipe have two houses, each in a different part of the city.

They also have a dog called Paco, so I bring Lucas with me whenever I visit. Lucas plays with his dog cousin while I play with my human cousins.

Paco loves eating toys and *zapatos*. Good thing that when Lucas is with him, he's busy enough playing chase to forget about his love for chewing shoes and other things.

Cami is older than me, and she has probably read every book in the *biblioteca*. When we have sleepovers, she retells the stories she's read. Even if they're a little scary and I ask her to skip the most frightening parts because Lucas won't like them, all the stories are ***fascinantes.*** She even taught me what the word ***fascinante*** means, so I know her stories are ***fascinantes.***

Pipe is younger than me. He's the best inventor and builder I know. Together we build imaginary worlds, like secret underground caves or deep-sea stations.

Pipe and I have gotten into trouble a number of times.

There was a time at my apartment when we decided, while brushing our teeth, to investigate how much weight the sink could hold. Turns out, the sink cannot hold

as much weight as we thought.

Mami had to call the plumber to fix the sink. She made Pipe and me mop and clean the whole bathroom.

While I like spending time with Piti and with Cami and Pipe and Paco, the person I like to spend time with the most is Mami. Unfortunately, like I said, things have been changing. Lately, Mami has been spending a lot of time elsewhere. Without me. A. LOT.

# CHAPTER 4

Mami has a new friend. His name is Luis. Luis is the reason I'm spending so much more *tiempo* with relatives and less with Mami. These are some things I know about Luis. So far.

(I know all this because Mami has told me about Luis. Okay, maybe she didn't tell me that his beard is prickly, but what beard isn't prickly?)

I should have known the moment I saw Mami's new hairstyle that we were in *problemas*.

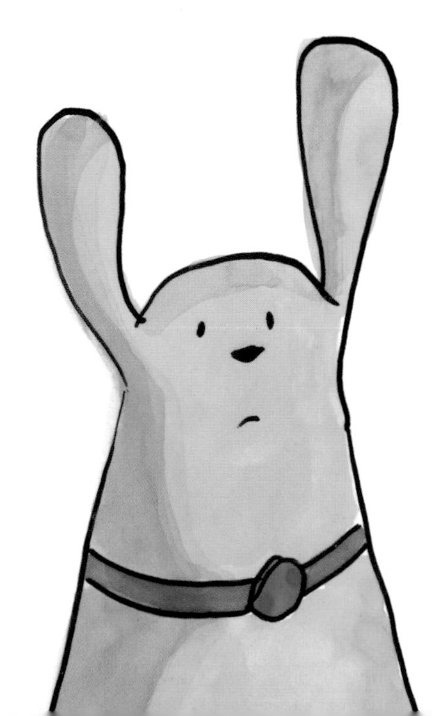

The first time I met Luis, he asked if I like taking pictures. Of course I like taking pictures! Especially pictures of Lucas. Who doesn't like taking pictures?

He asked if I like music. Of course I like music.

Luis asked if I like animals. I found it odd that he would ask such a question in front of Lucas!

Mami said I should have answered yes instead of shrugging. I think perhaps he could have asked fewer *preguntas*.

# *Adults ask strange questions.*
# VERY STRANGE.

Here are a few examples:

**What do you want to be when you grow up?**
My answer would be, I'm too busy being a kid to know what I'll do in a billion years!

**Do you *really* like *repollitas*? I've never met a kid who likes *repollitas*!**
My answer would be, Why wouldn't every kid LOVE Brussels sprouts? They are absolutely delicious and tiny and cute.

**Why can't you be quiet?**
My answer would be, Because I am alive and I make noises, even when I don't want to. Even when I'm just sitting and breathing, I make noises through my nose as air goes by.

**Why don't you like to wear dresses?**
My answer would be, Girls who want to climb trees without scraping their knees and girls who want their legs to be warm would much rather wear pants.

**So, is Lucas your friend?**
My answer would be, He's not just my friend.

He is absolutely-
no-question-
hands-down
my best
of *amigos.*
Period.

# CHAPTER 5

Another thing I learned about Luis is that he likes jazz and has a big music collection. We listen to his music when we drive to La Finca, his country house.

He goes there on weekends and sometimes invites Mami and me to come along. As it turns out,

I *like* jazz!

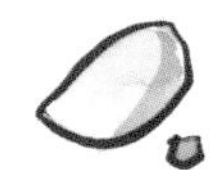

*And I like La Finca.*

REALLY LIKE IT.

Here's why:

It is cooler than in the city, so the AIR always smells fresh and crisp.

There are two HORSES and a DONKEY and DOGS and GEESE and SHEEP and some COWS; I haven't counted how many.

Luis makes FRESH CHEESE with milk from his cows. The cheese tastes great with HOT CHOCOLATE, especially late in the afternoon.

Mami doesn't mind if I get grass stains on my shirt's elbows or cow manure on my boots. It's okay to get MESSY while at La Finca.

Most important, LUCAS LOVES LA FINCA.

PASTELES DOÑA ROSA
BUÑUELOS
EMPANADAS
REPAS
UGOS

Luis's country house is in a small town called Tenjo. The road trip is long enough to have to stop and eat a snack, like crunchy *empanadas* or soft and delicious *buñuelos* on our way there. But it's also short enough that we don't have to travel for days to get there.

Luis gave me a camera to take pictures. He is a very good photographer and has been showing me how to take pictures of *"cosas interesantes."* Sometimes I think he's right about what to take pictures of. But I don't see what is so interesting about shadows or running water. I'd much rather take pictures of Lucas playing ball.

I like the camera and I like the visits to thc farm and I think Luis is a nice person, but sometimes I wish it were just me and Mami and Lucas, like before. Sometimes I would like to rewind time and let Mami and Luis be just *amigos*. We could go to La Finca every now and then and take a few photographs here and there, but perhaps not own a camera, and not have to share Mami with him EVERY DAY.

## CHAPTER 6

Cami has heard about La Finca and says she'd like to go there with me and Mami and Luis sometime. Luis has said that maybe someday she can, and Pipe, too.

Cami says maybe Mami will marry Luis. I'm not sure I like it when Cami says that. Cami says maybe I'll get to be a flower girl. I don't like that, either.

I don't want to be a flower girl.

I just want to be myself!

*Being a flower girl would be the worst.*
THE. WORST.
And here's why:

A flower girl has to parade down the aisle while every single person at the wedding watches her every move.

A flower girl has to pretend she likes throwing flower petals very delicately. There's zero fun in that.

She has to wear a stiff dress, and there's not a chance that wouldn't be itchy!

She also has to stay quiet and not ask any questions during the whole *ceremonia*.

She has to stand and smile for pictures. Even if the *vestido* itches or she has questions to ask or she is tired or bored.

Abue said that Mami won't ever stop being my *mami,* even if she does get married again.

I'm glad Abue said that. I was able to think about nicer things and stop worrying about anyone getting married (*especialmente* Mami)!

He also said that I most definitely wouldn't have to be a flower girl if I didn't want to be, and that has been one big relief.

I don't think Mami will want to marry Luis. I don't think Mami will want to get married at all! Mami is just my *mami*. Why would she need to get married, anyway?

# CHAPTER 7

Sometimes I can't help but wonder what life would be like if my dad were still alive.

I know very little about my dad. VERY LITTLE. He died in a fire when I was a tiny baby.

I do know that Mami was very sad for a long time.

# *Here's what else I know:*

My dad's name was Jaime,
but people called him Jimmy.

He was a phenomenal
basketball player.

Like me, Dad was a big soccer fan. He really liked watching Pelé play *fútbol.*

Unlike me, my dad was very good at math. That's why he became an engineer. (I know for sure I won't become an engineer!)

My dad's hair was very curly. Mine only curls when it's very hot outside.

I don't like it when it's Father's Day and they ask us to make crafts for fathers at school, but not everything can be the way I want it to be. I just wish teachers knew that, for me, it would be okay not to make cards to "The Best *Papá* Ever." I usually just change the letters a little and write my card to "The Best *Perro* Ever." Lucas certainly appreciates that.

It makes me sad not to have known my dad.

I wish I could hold his hand.

I wish he were here to help me fix things
when they break.

I wish he were here when I'm sad because my team
lost another *fútbol* game,
    or to celebrate birthdays,
        or to take Lucas for long walks with me.

I often wonder what he smelled like,
    and if he liked to laugh,
        and if his voice was soft like Abue's
            or loud like Mr. Tompkins's.

I'm sure he would have liked to be with me and, sometimes, knowing that is good enough.

# CHAPTER 8

I wish I were right about Mami not wanting to get married. As it turns out, she and Luis ARE getting married. They told me so one day while we were eating ice cream. I was so distraught, my appetite went away.

My appetite had never gone away before. My *helado* melted and became one big chocolate-flavored puddle.

I don't know how this marriage thing with Luis will work out.

Will Mami marrying Luis mean he'll move in with us?

And does this mean I will see Luis every day?

Will he use my shampoo on his beard?

Who will make breakfast now?

And what about my rock collection? Will I have to get rid of it to make room for his things?

Where will he put his clothes?

And does this mean jazz will be playing ALL. THE. TIME. at home?

So many questions. So many mysteries!

Mami says the wedding won't happen until January, so there are still a few months to figure things out. She says that I won't have to give up my rocks and that she'll keep making breakfast, as usual.

I don't think things will be as simple as Mami makes them sound. There's no way someone and ALL of his THINGS can come to live with us without life changing a lot!

As it turns out, I won't need to move just a few of my things. I will need to move ALL of my things. ALL. OF. THEM. We're packing everything, *todo,* and moving to a new place.

I'm liking this idea of marriage less and less. Even my neighbors, my *ventanas*, and my doorbell are changing. Right now, it's all one big chaotic mess. At this rate, I'll have to make sure the movers don't put Lucas in a box!

Mr. Tompkins has said I have to focus more in class. I haven't even been able to play *fútbol*.

I'm too distracted by the idea of moving away from my home and my bedroom, from where I can see the Andes Mountains day and night.

# CHAPTER 10

Abuelita has called on her seamstress, Clarita, to make Mami's dress. I didn't know Clarita could make wedding dresses; I just thought she hemmed my school uniform.

It turns out, Clarita has a lot of experience making fancy dresses! She showed us pictures of the many she's made. I am not a fan of dresses, but I had to tell Clarita that she's so good at making them beautiful, even I might consider wearing one.

I just wish I hadn't said that aloud. Right away, Mami and Abuelita asked Clarita to take my measurements.

I didn't like that one bit. Clarita had me stand on an apple box, wearing only my underwear. I had to stand as still as a statue while she wrapped me in measuring tape, yelling numbers at her assistant to jot down. I told Mami and Abuelita that I wasn't getting married and that there was no reason for me to have a dress, much less to be standing still like an *estatua* for hours wearing only my underwear!

Abuelita said it would not take hours and that once we were done with the measurements, we'd all go get hot chocolate with *queso*. So I put up with the dressmaking session. Sometimes sacrifices must be made in order to enjoy some chocolate in any form or shape.

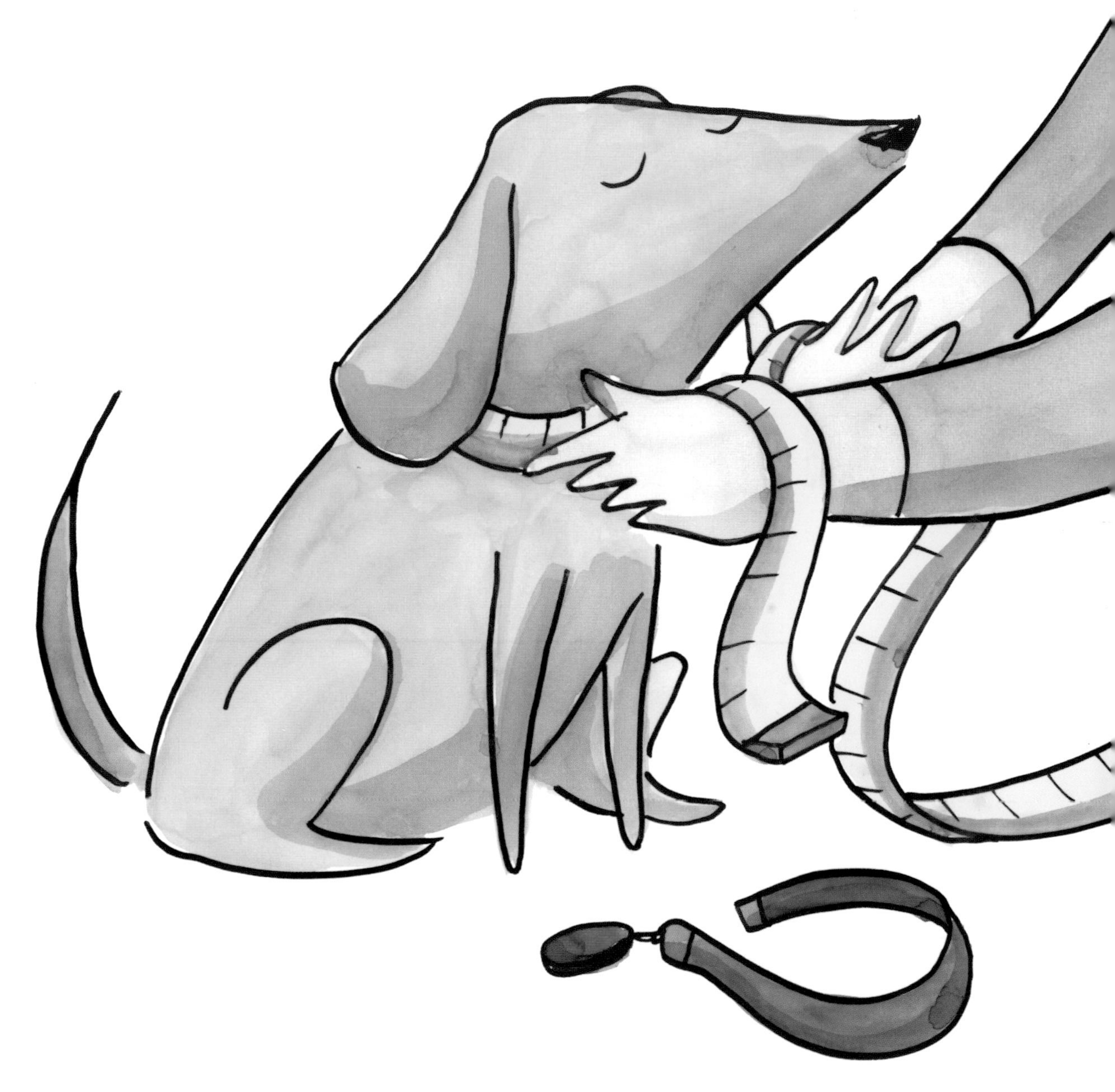

Clarita also made Lucas a special bow tie. I'm not sure he'll be too happy about that, but at least we'll all be wearing something special for Mami's new wedding.

Piti will be making Mami's wedding cake because she is—besides Mami—the best baker I know.

She has started trying different recipes, and I'm helping her by being the judge of them. Lucas and I taste every sample as it comes right out of the oven. We've even tasted some more than once so we can tell Piti with full certainty which one is the very best. If all weddings need a cake judge, I think I might want to grow up to be a professional one. This is a job I can do very, very well!

# CHAPTER 11

I have to admit, the *casa* we'll be moving into is really nice. There are lots of great things about it. There's a backyard for Lucas to run around in and plenty of space for my entire rock collection. There's also a nice balcony that will be the perfect place for Lucas and me to do some stargazing at night and some city-spotting during the day.

I've also noticed, during our trips back and forth between the old apartment and the new *casa,* that my *abuelos'* house isn't too far. That is a very, very good thing. And I will still be going to the same school, which is a **BIG** relief. And Mami has said that once we move out of our apartment, we'll still visit our dear neighbors, the Sheldons, and the Herrera brothers at their shop.

There are so many things being brought to the new *casa* that we have to jump in and help the movers. Luis moves the heavy boxes in. Lucas and I help Mami figure out where things will go, and we help put things away.

There are bookshelves everywhere, and there are big windows that fill the place with light, which Mami's plants will like.

Later, Lucas and I explore our neighborhood-to-be. Thanks to his incredible ability to smell things, we've already found a great bakery, a mango stand, and a very big park.

Although most of our stuff is now in the new *casa,* we won't move in until after the wedding. I'm glad. This means we have time to say good-bye to our old apartment slowly.

I will forever miss my old home. Bogotá will never look the same as from my old bedroom window. Fortunately, Luis has shown me how the Andes Mountains and the city lights can be seen from the balcony in the new house—I can even see Monserrate from here!

## CHAPTER 12

In September, it felt like the wedding was still far into the future. Suddenly the end of January is less than a week away! Mami's dress is ready, and so is mine. Clarita did a great job making it as comfortable as a dress can be, which still isn't too comfortable, but isn't as itchy as my uniform and should be fine for one day. Then I can go back to wearing pants.

A few days later, Piti's cake is ready! She has to put it up somewhere really high in her kitchen for now so that her dogs can't get to it. If they did, they would eat it!

A day before the wedding, Mami asks me to go with her to her hair salon. I said maybe it would be a good idea to find a new hair salon, one that didn't try new things with her hair. She said maybe I could wear my hair differently for a change.

I don't think there's anything wrong with my hair. Pigtails suit me just fine. But Mami insists, and before I know it, I'm sitting on a huge chair with a gown tied around my neck and

surrounded by scissors and blow-dryers.

The hairdresser doesn't stop asking Mami about her wedding. In the mirror, Mami catches me rolling my eyes but doesn't say anything. I'm sure I'll be in trouble for it later, and then everything about this day will feel even worse.

Once we're done with the hair-torturing session and with making me look like I have a cabbage on each side of my head, we leave. To my surprise, Mami doesn't say anything about me rolling my eyes. Instead, she takes me out for ice cream. This time I don't let it melt.

While I eat, Mami tells me she loves me and that there's no one more important to her than me. She tells me that, no matter what, she'll always be there for me, to love me,

to take care of me,

to laugh with me,

and to cook my favorite food

of all foods, *repollitas.*

And I believe her, because Mami only says things she means.

This is the most refreshing ice-cream break in the history of ice-cream breaks. Not because of the mint chocolate-chip ice cream that didn't melt, but because Mami has explained that, just like she's my favorite person ever, I'm *her* favorite

person

ever.

# CHAPTER 13

My hair may look like a pair of big *buñuelos* and my dress might be too cold for this rainy twenty-sixth of January, but that's okay. The wedding isn't half as bad as I imagined.

Mami looks beautiful, and Luis doesn't look bad at all.

There are beautiful flower arrangements, but no need for flower girls, which is great. There's a seat for me in the front row and right next to it, some space for Lucas.

Mami and Luis look happy, and the ceremony goes swiftly. I don't even yawn once.

Faster than I can count all the people who are there, Mami and Luis are married.

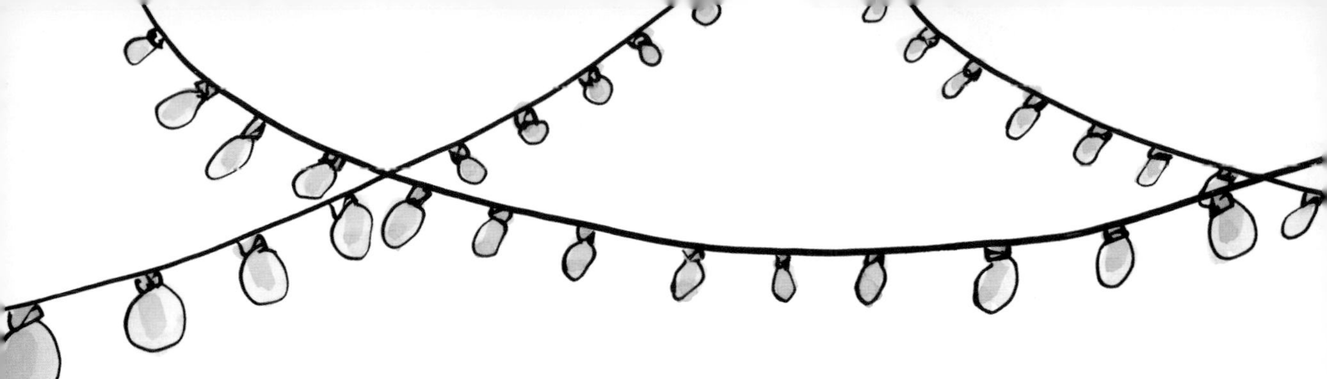

So many of the people I love came: my *abuelos,* Piti, Pipe and Cami, Tía Cris, the Sheldons, and Memo. The Herrera brothers, too! And my good friend Juli.

I'm glad that Luis suggested I bring my camera! Now I can take pictures of my old *familia* and my big new family.

It's all so nice that time flies! Once we are done with Mami and Luis saying *I do,* and people are done posing for pictures and eating Piti's delicious cake, Lucas, Mami, Luis, and I go to our new home.

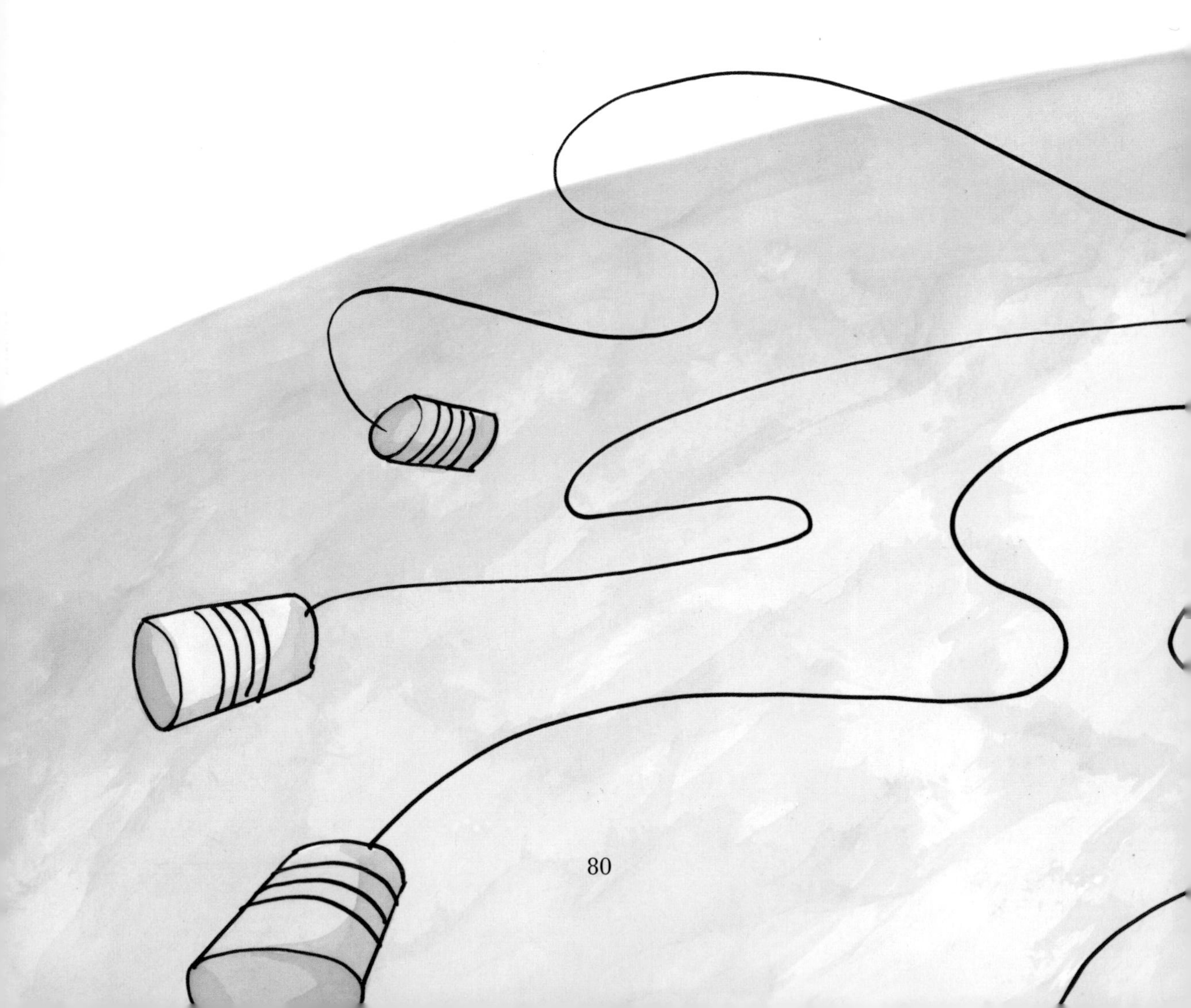

AR5
BOGOTÁ, DC

At our new *casa,* I get out of my dress and put on my comfy old pajamas. It wasn't easy to find them among all the boxes around the house! I finally found them in a big one labeled *esenciales de Juana.* I would have thought that markers, books, and the flashlight Abue gave me last year were essentials. Perhaps even my soccer ball and cleats would have made it into my most-important-box-in-life, but . . . pajamas! Who could have ever thought of those?

Fortunately, Lucas doesn't wear pajamas. He only needs to take off his bow tie to go back to being his good old self.

There might still be boxes in every room and there is clearly A LOT left to do to make this feel like home, but, I must say, it feels pretty good so far.

I think I will probably hang up some of the pictures I took at the wedding on the newly painted walls of my bedroom. They will help me remember my old neighbors, my cousins, my *abuelos,* and Piti. Maybe I'll even put up one of me and my old *amigo* Lucas all dressed up! And I will hang some photos of all the new people in my *familia,* too.

# *There are a lot!*

Pipe holding Paco!

Here's Cami.

My *abuelo* having a little extra cake

Tía Cris, wearing a gorgeous dress

Abuelita rearranging the flowers

Luis and Mami, very happy

Piti giving cake to Lucas

Perhaps having to share Mami with more people isn't all that bad. Plus I'm starting to really like the idea of more cousins and uncles and aunts: I'm thinking it might guarantee an adventure or two.

So many old and new things are now combined: my old shoes, my new dress; my old rocks, my new bedroom. My old *amigo* Lucas, my new *casa*.

*New* and *old* might not add up to *perfect,* but life is interesting and that, right now, seems much better than *perfección*.

JUANA MEDINA was born and grew up in Bogotá, Colombia. At school, she got into trouble for drawing cartoon versions of her teachers. Eventually, however, all that drawing (and trouble) paid off. Juana Medina is the author-illustrator of *Juana & Lucas,* which won the 2017 Pura Belpré Author Award. She is also the author-illustrator of the picture books *1 Big Salad, ABC Pasta,* and *Sweet Shapes,* and the illustrator of *Lena's Shoes Are Nervous: A First-Day-of-School Dilemma* by Keith Calabrese. Juana Medina lives with her family in Washington, D.C.

FRUTAS